This book belongs to

_____

A Forgotten Island in Hawaii

Book 1
The Adventures of T-Naya, Tamara, Tegan & Talia

Y'vonne Clements

ISBN 978-0-6486041-0-5 (print)
ISBN 978-0-6486041-1-2 (ebook)

A Forgotten Island in Hawaii
Y'vonne Clements

First edition: 2023

Edited by: Crystal Leonardi, Bowerbird Publishing
Interior Design by: Crystal Leonardi, Bowerbird Publishing
Front Cover Concept & Design by: Charlotte Dixon
Rear Cover Concept & Design: Crystal Leonardi, Bowerbird Publishing
Illustrations: Y'vonne Clements (AINight Cafe), Linda Schan, Blueys Photography

Distributed by Bowerbird Publishing
Available in National Library of Australia

Crystal Leonardi, Bowerbird Publishing
Julatten, Queensland, Australia
www.crystalleonardi.com

Dedicated to my granddaughter, T-Naya.

With love, from Nanna.

Contents

Chapter 1

Basking under the warm Hawaiian sun, Tracey perched on a mossy rock, nestled amid the enchanting waters of a magical island. Her mind buzzed with curiosity about the wild adventures her four teenage friends were brewing today. With a gleeful splash, she dove into the ocean's gentle embrace, descending deeper and deeper into the realm

where mermaids slept within iridescent pearl shells. Those mermaids, adorned in shimmering pearls and colourful, sparkly stones, looked like they were plucked from dreams.

As the day awakened, T-Naya was the first to stir. Her pearl shell unfurled, revealing a treasure chest of glistening pearls. With a joyful twirl, she swam playfully, awaiting her sisters' emergence - Talia, Tegan, and Tamara.

Their underwater world was a carnival of sea creatures, always ready to play games and dart in and out of the sweeping swirls of T-Naya's tail. Laughter filled the water as some mischievous creatures sought refuge in her golden-blonde hair.

Today, they decided to don their elegant blue scales. As Talia and Tegan joined T-Naya, they shimmered like the sea itself, their long, jet-black hair flowing alongside. The twins loved matching outfits, partly to bewilder the wise old mermaids.

Tamara, their youngest sister, always emerged last. They playfully rapped on her pearl shell until she stirred from her slumber.

Their life beneath the sea was a fairy tale come to life. The mermaids constantly discovered new nooks and crannies for adventure. Now that they were growing up, they relished their newfound independence.

With Tamara finally stirring, she combed her flowing auburn hair with a black onyx comb. To match her sisters, she, too, chose the blue scales. The four mermaids swam gracefully to the surface, embracing the brilliant sunshine. They laughed and played with the amiable sea creatures who enjoyed games and greeted them with friendly waves. A school of playful dolphins appeared nearby, and the mermaids couldn't help but wonder why these dolphins weren't scared of humans like they were. Frightened by the thought of humans capturing their ancestors, the mermaids quickly retreated beneath the waves.

The dolphins confided in them, revealing that humans fed them, creating a bond of trust. T-Naya cautioned her sisters to stay hidden beneath the water or behind rocks, corals, and seaweed.

Tamara, always the adventurer, suggested they explore the island's other side. Talia and Tegan eagerly agreed, and T-Naya led the way. On the island's far side, the water was delightfully warmer, and seaweed swayed gently in the waves. Sometimes, they'd float to the surface to bask in the summer sun's warmth. But they had to be careful, watching out for fishing nets left out by the humans. Even the whales weren't spared from human intrigue, and tales circulated of humans trying to catch mermaids!

As their playful swim continued, exhaustion slowly crept in. The journey to the other side of the island was a long one, and they knew they were growing tired. They came across an old shipwreck on the ocean floor, a place they loved to explore and play.

But then, a sudden realisation struck them. As they swam to the surface, their eyes met another shipwreck, this time on the beach. It dawned on them that they had ventured too far and were now caught in powerful waves. Worried and uneasy, they all agreed that returning to the safety of the ocean floor was the wisest choice, where they could resume their joyful play with the sea creatures.

The mermaids, sharp observers of the world above, noted the sky's changing colours. It was a sign that the moon would soon emerge, casting its enchanting glow. Dark storm clouds began to obscure the once-bright sun, turning the water around them cold and murky. As the seas grew and the storm approached, the mermaids found them-selves unexpectedly close to the beach again.

Inquisitively, Tamara poked her head above the waterline to survey their surroundings, and her eyes fell upon the shipwreck once more. This time, she also saw a sailboat crash onto the shore and spotted a lone human swimming in the water. Frightened, she quickly hid be-hind a nearby rock, but it was too late; the human had seen her. To her surprise, he mimicked the dolphins' friendly gestures to greet her.

T-Naya acted swiftly, pulling Tamara back beneath the water's surface, fearful of the human. However, a strange fascination gripped Tamara's heart, and she decided to swim closer to the shore to explore further. Her sisters called out in concern, fearing for their safety.

Tamara ventured deeper beneath the waves and continued to approach the human. Returning to the surface, she saw the human swimming toward her. The storm clouds had now cleared, allowing the sun to illuminate her shimmering scales, making her glisten like a jewel in the sea. Nearby, some playful dolphins caught her attention, and she inquired about the human's identity. The dolphins assured her that he was a kind soul who had played with them before. Relieved, Tamara decided it was time to rejoin her sisters and make their way back home, leaving behind the fascinating encounter for another day.

Chapter 2

The very next day, the entire mermaid clan joined Tamara in her quest to meet the friendly human once more. As they reached the far side of the island, her sisters gracefully submerged beneath the surface,

leaving Tamara perched courageously on a rock, scanning the horizon.

Soon enough, her sharp eyes caught sight of the human. He began making sounds she recognised from other humans, filling her heart with a hint of fear. In a sudden rush of uncertainty, she dove into the water and swam away, but the human's cry stopped her in her tracks.

"Please don't leave me. I'm all alone!" he pleaded.

T-Naya, Tegan, and Talia felt anxious for their sister but refused to abandon her. Tamara returned to the rock, determined to communicate with the human with the help of some friendly dolphins. Her sisters, with great care, swam underneath her, guiding Tamara into the safety of the deeper waters.

Tamara had no choice but to return home with her sisters. Although they were angry with her for allowing the human to see her, the human's enchanting plea left Tamara deeply captivated.

As the mermaids made their way home, the setting sun painted the sky in vivid hues. They were still upset with Tamara for putting them in danger, emphasising the importance of always returning long before the moon's rise. Upon their return, they shared their daring adventure with Tracey, who listened with scepticism. She couldn't believe what they recounted about Tamara's encounter with the human. Unwilling to back down, Tamara asked her sister to return with her the following day.

The three beautiful mermaids, exhausted from the day's events, chose not to argue further. They nodded in agreement, opened their pearl shells, and nestled in for a peaceful night's sleep.

Chapter 3

As the first rays of the morning sun touched the water, the mermaids began to stir from their slumber. T-Naya was the first to open her pearl shell, wondering if her sisters were already awake. She found Talia and Tegan up and about, helping each other with their shiny black hair, and selecting their outfits for the day. She joined in, carefully choosing something to wear.

But as they got ready, a realisation struck them like a splash of cold water—Tamara had not emerged from her pearl shell yet. T-Naya, concerned, tapped the shell, but there was no response. With a mix of confusion and worry, she slowly opened the shell and discovered it was empty—Tamara was nowhere to be found! The commotion reached Tracey's ears, and she hurried to see what was wrong. T-Naya asked her if Tamara had mentioned her plans, but she hadn't, and no one had heard her leave.

With deepening concern, Tracey enlisted the help of other mermaids, inquiring about Tamara's whereabouts. None had seen her. The mermaid sisters quickly set off in pairs to question turtles and sea creatures, but no one had any information about Tamara's disappearance. In response, Tracey organised a search party, a determined effort to find her.

T-Naya, Talia, and Tegan feeling responsible for their sister's absence, left a note for Tracey, explaining their plan to return to the sunken shipwreck, hoping to find Tamara there. When they arrived at the site, they encountered a pod of friendly dolphins, who informed them they had seen Tamara heading towards the shipwreck on the shore, making her way to the hidden rocks beneath the waves.

With fortune on their side, the waves were gentle that day, and the current mild, making their swim to the rocks safe. They discovered Tamara where they had expected her to be, perched on the rocks. Reluctant to surface, they called out to her and then quickly retreated to the safety of the water. T-Naya asked the dolphins to fetch Tracey.

Beneath the surface, they could hear the human from the previous day making sounds, leaving them wondering what it all meant. When Tracey arrived and found Tamara so close to the human, she couldn't help but feel astonished. She couldn't fathom why the human hadn't harmed or captured Tamara. Anxious that it might be a trick, she urged the dolphins to swim to the shore to get Tamara's attention.

The dolphins agreed and invited Tamara to play with them in the water as they approached the shore.

Basking on a rock, Tamara continued her conversation with the human, aided by the dolphins. But when the dolphins signalled her and conveyed the message that the mermaids were searching for her, she dove into the water and swam out to join them. She tried to explain to her sisters that the human meant no harm, but they didn't believe her.

Reluctantly, Tamara agreed to return to her pearl shell. Tracey, T-Naya, Talia, and Tegan were overjoyed that she was safe, but they implored her not to vanish again and to stay away from the human.

"He plays like we do, and he seems lonely. There are no other humans on the island. I'm not scared of him," Tamara insisted, her heart torn between the enchanting world of the human and her family's concerns.

T-Naya began to wonder if Tamara might be right about the human, and she suggested they consult King Neptune, the ruler of the ocean, to learn the truth about the humans and their intentions.

Chapter 4 🐚

The following day, the sun rose early, casting a golden glow over the ocean. The mermaid sisters frolicked with their sea creature friends on the ocean floor. Sea flowers danced in harmony with the tide, and the sun's gentle rays shimmered across the water's surface. Surprisingly, Tamara, who was typically the last to awaken, was already dressed in her shimmering scales. Her long, glossy hair was neatly brushed, and they were all eager to set out and visit King Neptune.

The older mermaids overheard their excited chatter and arrived to offer some guidance. They reminded the young mermaids to use their best manners when visiting the King and explained how to find his palace nestled among the vibrant corals. T-Naya suggested asking the dolphins to show them the way. The dolphins were found playfully swimming alongside boats, delighting humans with their tricks. With joy, the dolphins invited the mermaids to jump on their backs for a ride to King Neptune's palace.

Holding on tightly to their dolphin guides, the mermaids squealed with delight as they raced through coral gardens and swayed through seaweed forests. Along the way, they encountered turtles and playful octopuses, exchanging waves and laughter. The dolphins relished showing off their skills, leaping in and out of the water, with the mermaids riding along.

Upon their arrival at an unusual part of the ocean, the mermaids were exhausted and sought refuge on some rocks to catch their breath and fix their hair. Here, they observed unfamiliar sea creatures of all shapes, sizes, and colours, and the seaweed had a strange appearance. In this part of the ocean, colours seemed to shift and change—the water, their scales, and even their hair transformed.

As they took a break, more mermaids arrived, having been trapped in human nets. They wanted to hear about Tamara's experience and consult King Neptune to verify its truth. The grand stairway to the palace loomed before them. Swimming up to the palace doors, they knocked, and a large, brightly coloured seahorse opened the door, instructing them to follow the hallway to reach the King.

T-Naya, the boldest among them, entered first, with her fellow mermaids following in line. The palace was adorned with tiaras, colourful stones, coral, and shells—it was a breathtaking sight. As they reached the end of the hallway, they encountered a door concealed by seaweed. The seahorse opened it and gestured for them to enter. Inside, a towering merman sat atop a grand rock. His deep voice resonated, "Hello, please, have a seat."

King Neptune wore a magnificent crown, and his hair was long, flowing, and sparkling, much like the mermaids'. He even had hair on his face, an entirely new concept to the mermaids. The King's presence enthralled them, rendering them momentarily speechless. Then, King Neptune's laughter filled the room, and the mermaids began to relax. He was friendly and kind, even though he was enormous.

T-Naya, finally finding her voice, posed a question to him, "Can you share the stories of our ancestors and the humans?" Tamara recounted her experience with the human she had made friends with through the dolphins and how he seemed lonely. King Neptune found it extraordinary that a human could be alone but cautioned Tamara that it could be a trap.

"You must never trust humans," he warned.

King Neptune dispatched the dolphins to investigate the human further and learn more about his intentions. The mermaids agreed with this course of action and were eager to return home to share King Neptune's decision with Tracey and the others. The dolphins kindly offered to provide them with a ride back, and soon they were back home.

After recounting their day to Tracey and the others, Tegan and Talia frolicked in a sunken ship with their sea creature friends, playfully trying on tiaras, necklaces, and sunken treasures, pretending they were in a palace like King Neptune's.

As evening approached, Tamara pondered the human she had encountered, wondering about their next encounter but well aware of the dangers. Perhaps the dolphins could help her again, she wondered.

Chapter 5

When morning broke, the sun remained hidden behind heavy, dark clouds. The sky turned a sombre grey, and the rain pelted the water's surface with intensity. Lightning streaked across the sky, followed by thunderous roars that stirred the mermaids from their sleep.

Realising they'd have to remain close to home due to the stormy weather, the mermaids decided to engage in some indoor fun—playing dress-up. Tracey unveiled a massive pearl shell brimming with dazzling jewellery, tiaras, shiny stones, and colourful dangles meant for their hair. They took turns brushing each other's hair and adorning it with ribbons and delicate sea flowers.

However, Tamara lingered in her shell, feeling a tinge of sadness about missing out on adventures due to the weather. T-Naya attempted to lift her spirits, extending an invitation to join their dress-up game. She reassured Tamara that the dolphins would soon return with news about her human friend.

As the skies cleared, Tamara and T-Naya swam to the surface to check if the dolphins had returned. They managed to catch up with the dolphins just in time, as the dolphins were on their way back to King Neptune. The human had shared his story—a tale of being caught in a massive wave that sent his sailboat crashing into the rocks and onto the shore. He had lost sight of his friends and was reluctant to swim far due to the presence of sharks.

The mermaids felt a deep sense of empathy for the stranded human and wished to help him. The dolphins assured them that he was friendly. Their next step was to approach King Neptune, seeking his assistance in rescuing the human.

The mermaids swam back down to share the dolphins' message with the others. Tamara felt distraught, but the elder mermaids emphasised the importance of awaiting King Neptune's decision and respecting their wishes. T-Naya offered Tamara a loving hug, soothing her worries and promising that everything would turn out well.

As the sun began its descent, the mermaids gathered for their evening meal. The sun's warm, golden glow signalled that it was time to return to their pearl shells for a night's rest. In the quiet of their underwater abode, the young mermaids sent silent prayers for Tamara's human friend and snuggled into their shells for the night. T-Naya held a glimmer of hope that the human would remain safe until he could be rescued.

Chapter 6

The following day, everyone was up early, fully dressed and prepared for the day's important mission. Even the older mermaids were eager to assist the stranded human. Tamara and Tracey were the last to join the rest of the mermaids. They had decided on a plan: all the mermaids would check on the human with Tamara, while Tracey went to see King Neptune. Tamara couldn't contain her excitement!

As they set out, T-Naya called out to Tamara, urging her to slow down. She was swimming so fast, carried away by her anticipation. Tamara, in sheer delight, even playfully raced the dolphins to the other side of the island. It didn't take long before they heard the human calling out to Tamara. The mermaids cautiously ensured he was alone before emerging to the surface.

The human was thrilled to see Tamara and waved his arms in excitement, which initially startled the other mermaids. Tamara gracefully slid onto a rock and watched the human swim towards her. To everyone's surprise, a friendly shark swam past Tamara to ensure she was alright. He gave the human a stern look but left them be when Tamara assured him she was okay.

The human gazed in amazement at Tamara as he approached the rock, slowly realising that she was a mermaid. He had heard stories

but had never believed they were true. The other mermaids remained hidden but observed the human's genuine friendliness, even though they couldn't understand his language.

Meanwhile, Tracey returned with the dolphins, relaying King Neptune's instructions. She instructed the dolphins to approach the human and advise him to climb onto their backs. They would give him a ride to another human's boat. The mermaids hoped that this plan would safely return the human to his home.

The dolphins swam up to Tamara and revealed their plan, asking for her assistance since the human trusted her the most. She agreed and leaped onto one of the dolphin's backs, while another dolphin nudged the human to do the same. He glanced at Tamara's reassuring expression and decided to follow her lead. Gripping the dolphins tightly, they darted through the water like lightning, with Tamara and the human aboard.

Tracey and the young mermaids watched from behind the rocks and felt a surge of happiness seeing the human rescued. As they got closer to a boat, Tamara realised she couldn't be seen by other humans and would have to leave her friend. The dolphins began to slow down, and both Tamara and the human cried as they waved their goodbyes.

Tamara felt a deep sadness as she slipped off her dolphin and returned to the water. The human continued on the back of his dolphin, heading toward a boat. Other dolphins made playful noises and performed tricks to catch the attention of the humans on board. Spotting Izzy on a dolphin, they lowered a rope into the water. Izzy slid off the dolphin and swam to the boat, offering his heartfelt thanks to the dolphins for rescuing him. Tamara watched from a distance, a tinge of sadness for having to part ways with her human friend.

As the boat sailed away into the horizon, T-Naya tried to encourage Tamara to return home. Once the boat was out of sight, Tamara, T-Naya, Tracey, and all the other mermaids swam back to their underwater haven. They all wondered about the human's fate and hoped he was safe. As they nestled into their shells for the night, Tracey comforted Tamara by reminding her that tomorrow would bring new adventures. Tamara knew that she would never forget her human friend, Izzy.

Chapter 7

Izzy fondly recalls, "I was aboard a trawler, setting sail into the vast ocean. I had built a small sailing boat that I could tether to the trawler. The captain, a friend of my dad's, kindly allowed me to come along. When we reached our destination and dropped anchor, the crew helped me into my sailboat, and I set off into unknown waters. I was thrilled to be far from my island home, surrounded by the untouched coastlines of the Hawaiian Islands."

With enthusiasm, he continued, "I encountered some waves and thought they were manageable. But I miscalculated and drifted too close to the island. The waves grew larger and began pushing me toward a cove, where I saw them crashing into immense rocks along the beach. I tried to steer my boat, but I lost control. Before I knew it, my sailboat collided with the rocks and washed me onto the sandy shores."

Izzy described his survival, saying, "My boat began taking on water, and I noticed the damage to the hull. I recall waking up as the sun was setting, feeling the cold, damp sand beneath me. I was scared and had a pounding headache. I began building a fire, hoping it would signal my location to the trawler. Eventually, the waves carried my boat out to sea, but I managed to salvage matches, some food, a book, my jacket, and a length of rope."

The crew couldn't believe Izzy's luck in surviving. He continued, "I hoped someone would come looking for me soon. It was dark and chilly, so I attempted to keep warm by the fire, sheltered by a structure I built from branches and foliage I found on the beach. As the tide changed, my sailboat returned to the shore, and I fell asleep by the fire."

"The warmth of the sunrise dried my clothes, which had hung by the fire all night. With limited food and water, I decided to explore the island. I discovered coconuts on the ground and fruits in the trees. I felt relieved as I found more berries and collected them in my shirt, following my path back to the beach. Opening a coconut to enjoy its milk and flesh became a priority."

Feeling nourished and invigorated, Izzy embarked on further exploration of the island. He marvelled at the creatures he encountered, from lizards to colourful birds in the trees. Initial apprehension at the unfamiliar sounds around him gave way to an understanding that it was just the island's creatures moving about.

Soon, the sound of a waterfall reached Izzy's ears. His heart raced as he pushed through the trees and came upon a clearing that revealed a grand waterfall cascading into a sparkling lagoon, teeming with fresh water. Behind the waterfall lay a lush, rainforest-covered mountain with fruit trees, including bananas!

Izzy took a refreshing swim in the lagoon and sought a way to transport the water back to his camp. He filled his pockets with berries and made his way to the banana trees. As he continued, another clearing appeared, with small bush huts. Izzy's heart raced once more, hoping to find company. Unfortunately, the huts seemed deserted, with old furniture inside, untouched for years.

Exploring each hut, Izzy discovered clay mugs, plates, cutlery, barrels, wooden crates, pots, beds, and a water-carrying bowl.

Izzy shared more of his story with the crew, saying, "I remembered I had a water bottle on my boat, which I could fill from the bowl. With my pockets filled with berries and the bowl brimming with water, I returned to the beach. It was late afternoon when I got back to my camp, so I rested for a while. As the sun set, I decided it was best to stay by the fire in case a ship or the trawler passed the island. I planned to return to the huts the next day."

Chapter 8

Izzy felt the warmth of the ocean waters as they lapped at his feet on the sandy shore. He longed for a refreshing swim but couldn't help but worry about sharks lurking beneath the waves.

Not far away, he spotted some rocks just below the surface. Beyond those rocks, he saw dolphins frolicking in the water. With no boats in sight on the distant horizon, Izzy decided to test the waters, carefully swimming closer to the rocks, all while keeping an eye out for any signs of sharks. He didn't venture too far and returned to the safety of the beach as the waves grew bigger, and fatigue set in. Back on the shore, he savoured coconuts and berries, his gaze fixed on the horizon, hoping for a boat to appear.

As the day warmed up, Izzy made preparations to light a fire for the approaching chilly night. In moments of solitude, he found comfort in

singing to himself. He knew that once the sun dipped below the horizon, the chances of rescue grew slimmer. He snuggled beneath palm fronds as the night fell, offering quiet prayers in the hope of being found the next day.

Every night, he dreamt of home and his mother's comforting cooking. Izzy, only 16 years old, grappled with loneliness and fear each night as he drifted to sleep on the solitary beach.

Chapter 9

Izzy eagerly shared his survival story with the crew, saying, "Each morning, when the sun painted the sky with its golden light, I'd wake up and start planning ways to make my camp even better. After discovering those huts, I decided to bring back some things to the beach to make my little camp cozier. This way, I'd only need to return to the lagoon for fresh water and delicious bananas.

One day, as the sun blazed down and the day got hotter, I explored a calm water inlet further down the beach. It was so warm that I couldn't resist taking a dip. While I was in the water, a pod of dolphins noticed me and swam over. I'd heard that dolphins were friendly, so I waved to them as they approached. In the shallow waters, they began playing and making noises that sounded like they were trying to talk to me. They even pushed me gently back onto the beach, like they were protecting me from something. Maybe it was a shark? I thanked them, and in response, they stood on their tails in the water, flapping their flippers in excitement. It felt like they understood me!"

But then, as the dolphins swam away, Izzy couldn't help but feel a sense of loneliness creeping in.

He continued, "After my dolphin encounter, I headed back to the huts, hoping to find food for the evening's fire. I collected what I needed and returned to the beach."

The crew listened with wide-eyed curiosity, but Izzy didn't want to reveal too much about the island, fearing they might venture there themselves and discover the mermaids.

"That night, I decided to build a massive bonfire closer to the shore, hoping a passing ship would spot it. I'd brought back some crates from the hut and found an old blanket inside one of them. After cleaning it up and drying it by the fire, I finally had a warm blanket to sleep under. I stacked up the timber and bits of old broken chairs, and I felt so proud of the size of my bonfire."

Izzy went on to share how he caught his very first fish, saying, "I used some old forks from the huts to craft a spear. I heated them in the fire until they were easy to bend and sharpen, and I shaped them by striking them with a rock. Satisfied with my creation, I headed to the lagoon to test it out. As I stepped into the water, something stirred, and right at my feet was a curious crab! I snatched it up, just like my dad taught me, and brought it back to my beach camp to cook for dinner later that night."

The crew was now full of questions, asking Izzy if he had considered building a raft. Izzy replied, "I did think about it, but those rocks in the cove and beyond made venturing into open water quite dangerous. I'd seen sharks when swimming out to the rocks, and I wasn't willing to take that risk. Fortunately, the dolphins were always close by and would join me on my swim back to the beach. I often played with them in the water, and they'd wave their flippers and jump out of the water above me."

Before long, Izzy recounted how he caught a fish using his makeshift spear and talked about saving the crab. "I wrapped my fish in banana leaves from near the huts and placed it in the fire, sprinkling some coals on top. As I waited for it to cook, I sang with joy. It was such a treat to have a proper dinner, and I could hear the distant melodies of whales singing along with my tune."

Chapter 10

Izzy excitedly shared the next part of his adventure, saying, "The very next day, I set off to the lagoon to fetch my morning supply of fresh water, just like I always did. But as I was returning to my camp, something extraordinary was happening. The dolphins, who often kept me company, were making more noise than usual. It got me curious, and I hurried down to the beach to see what was going on."

He continued, "As I got closer, I spotted a much larger dolphin swimming alongside my dolphin friends. This bigger dolphin seemed to be the leader. It felt like they were trying to tell me something. So, without hesitation, I decided to swim out to them. Normally, the dolphins would push me back to the safety of the beach, protecting me from any lurking sharks. But this time, something was different. They pushed me further out into the deep water."

Izzy's eyes sparkled with the memory as he shared, "As I reached the pod of dolphins, one of them swam right between my legs and gently lifted me above the water. I held on tight as this dolphin started racing toward the endless horizon. And then, something incredible happened – I saw a familiar sight! It was the trawler, way out in the distance. The dolphins were taking me back to safety!"

He went on, "With all the dolphins from the cove swimming beside us, they began to create a joyful commotion in the water. They splashed, danced, and made all sorts of cheerful noises. They were trying to grab the attention of the humans on the trawler, shouting, 'Hey, look at us!'

The crew was amazed by Izzy's story, and some even whispered their amazement to each other. Izzy was relieved that nobody asked if he had seen mermaids, ensuring their secret remained safe.

Chapter 11

As the mermaids grew older, they gained more freedom, able to explore as long as they returned home by sunset. This expanded their world, filled with new adventures, exciting places, and perhaps the possibility of making new friends.

One day, while they were swimming on a different side of the ocean, they heard a captivating melody, a beautiful song sung by a mermaid nearby. As they swam closer to this unfamiliar island, the enchanting voice grew louder. They were confident it was a mermaid, but T-Naya had concerns it might be a trap. To investigate, she ventured closer alone, promising to return if it indeed was a mermaid.

T-Naya ascended to the crest of the gentle waves to get a better view. Inside a cave, on a rock, she discovered a captivating mermaid who sang her heart out, her beautiful hair swaying in the ocean breeze.

However, the lyrics of the song reveal a heart-wrenching tale of losing someone dear to her. T-Naya returned to her fellow mermaids to relay what she had witnessed and heard.

The collective empathy of the mermaids suggested that the singing mermaid might be in deep sorrow, possibly yearning for company. This time, Tamara volunteered to approach her, as she could empathise with the profound sadness. The other mermaids agreed and followed Tamara as they approached the cave.

Tamara gently surfaced near the cave's entrance and tenderly greeted the singing mermaid. The mermaid momentarily ceased her song to identify the source of the soft voice. She responded with a welcoming smile, inviting Tamara to join her on the rock. Tamara was delighted and asked if it was ok to bring three more mermaids. The mermaid's smile brightened further as she readily agreed.

Tamara summoned the others, and they emerged from the water simultaneously, evoking laughter from the singing mermaid as she saw the group. She gestured to them to find seats on the rocks. She introduced herself as Melody and inquired about their names, also expressing curiosity about their family.

Though the mermaids politely declined the offer of food, they inquired if Melody had any other family members. This question stirred emotions, and Melody tearfully revealed that her friend had ventured out a long time ago and had not returned. Melody also explained that she was responsible for two young mermaids, Macey and Molly, who sorely missed their friend, Mariah. The mermaids felt deep sympathy for her and temporarily set aside their own concerns. They discussed the possibility of providing support. Tamara suggested checking on the young mermaids, Macey and Molly and asked if they could accompany her. The mermaids followed Tamara as they swam through the cave, revealing a breathtaking entrance that led to a beautiful, shimmering, sunlit lagoon.

Chapter 12 🐚

At first, they observed nothing, continuing further along the sandy shoreline. The next time they surfaced, they spotted something vibrant. Swimming to investigate, they were amazed to discover a mermaid entangled in a net.

Without hesitation, they dragged her into the water, and a concerted effort was made to free her from the net. She made a faint noise, prompting them to persist. After painstaking efforts, they successfully freed her, pulling her beneath the ocean's surface. Anxiously, they awaited signs of life from her, fearing they might have arrived too late. Slowly, she began to stir but remained too weak to speak. They held her close, offering support.

She introduced herself as Mariah, and she voiced her concern for her missing friend. They consoled her, assuring her they had been searching for her and that Melody, Macey, and Molly were in good spirits. As Mariah recounted her ordeal, it became evident that she had ventured out to collect special seagrass for Macey and Molly when a trawler ship dropped its net on her and the other sea creatures.

Tracey and Tasha reacted with gasps upon hearing this harrowing account. Mariah went on to describe how the net had entrapped them, dragging them along the ocean floor. Eventually, they felt the effects of a violent storm above the water's surface, causing distress among all the trapped creatures. Some managed to escape during the turbulence, while a swordfish arrived, endeavouring to free them.

Amid the chaos, the swordfish began cutting the net, allowing several smaller creatures to break free. However, the net began to ascend just as Mariah was about to gain her freedom, trapping her once more. She recalled the net's quick ascent as a massive wave hit, sending everyone into a whirlpool. Eventually, she ended up in the cove, unable to make herself heard amidst the raging storm. She drifted in and out of consciousness, trapped within the unforgiving net.

Marina, Tracey, and Tasha assured her they would safely return her home. However, they were unsure about which way to go. They decided to surface briefly to check for the presence of dolphins. As they emerged from the water, Teenie, the helpful fish who had guided them earlier, was waiting, recognising that they had found the missing mermaid. She volunteered to lead them back to Mariah's home. Proceeding slowly and cautiously, they followed Teenie, staying low to avoid detection by any passing ships.

Along the way, they paused to inform the sea creatures that they had found Mariah. A group of dolphins approached, offering assistance, but Mariah hesitated, expressing her desire to travel at a slower pace. The dolphins volunteered to head to King Neptune to inform him that the search parties could be called off. Finally, just before the sun began to set, the sound of Melody's song reached their ears, signalling the proximity of Mariah's home.

As they entered the cave, they encountered Teenie, the helpful fish, for one last time. The mermaids said their goodbyes and continued into the cave. The sight of Melody with Mariah brought tears to their eyes. Macey and Molly swam over, overjoyed at the reunion, showering Mariah with hugs and kisses.

Chapter 13

The mermaids decided to give them some space to reconnect and catch up. They needed to return home, and with grateful words, they bid farewell to Mariah, Melody, Macey, Molly, and Teenie.

Tracey and Tasha faced uncertainty about their route home. However, their trusted friend Teenie appeared once again, offering to guide them back to familiar waters. They followed her carefully, remaining low in the water to avoid being seen by any potential ships.

Upon reaching the area they recognised, they thanked Teenie and an electric eel that helped light their way. When they spotted the sunken ship, they knew they were almost home. They expressed their gratitude to Teenie and the eel for their help.

Arriving at their homes, they found their family and fellow sea creatures waiting. The relieved and curious friends had gathered, eager to hear the details of their mission. T-Naya and Tamara were the first to emerge from their shells, overwhelmed with joy that Mariah had been found.

As the mermaids and sea creatures came together, the conversation was punctuated with excitement, shared tales, and gratitude. Tracey approached T-Naya, suggesting that she accompany them to visit King Neptune the following day. She believed that T-Naya's insights could be instrumental in ensuring the safety of the mermaids. T-Naya embraced the idea, and they sealed the evening within their shells, looking forward to the significant day ahead.

- THE END -

Acknowledgements

I would like to thank my husband, Billy, family and friends for their immense contributions, endless conversations, feedback and support.

To my circle of friends who have kept me in their prayers, when faith and trust were needed to continue my journey.

To my story readers, who supported and inspired me to keep writing. To all the children out there who need a place to lose themselves from the pressures of daily life. I hope 'The Forgotten Island in Hawaii' brings you the ability to fall asleep in a mystical fantasy world in the safest possible way.

To all the dolphins, turtles and sunsets who share the beautiful Hawaiian life. To the beautiful Hawaiian culture, MAHALO.

I'd also like to express my gratitude to my inspiring, creative publisher, Crystal Leonardi of Bowerbird Publishing. Crystal made the time to guide me through the mind field of publishing, whilst on immense time constrictions. I highly recommend Bowerbird Publishing to any writer like myself, who is just starting out. Crystal is an acclaimed award-winning author so understands from the writer's perspective, how daunting the publishing process can be.

To Jacquie Lait, Linda Schan, Jo King, David Pressley, Bob Sinclair, EL MA. Bohemian-beach-bug.

To Charlotte Dixon for her relentless work on my beautiful book cover.
To Blueys Photography for sharing his amazing pictures.

To my own mind, which helped me discover that when I focused on story writing, I became the character telling the story. I was able to forget reality, pain, worry and stress.

I hope I have succeeded for you all. Remember, every mountain you climb in this unpredictable world will give you strength to climb again.

Stay strong. Forge your own path; don't be a follower, be a great leader. This world needs more of them.

Y'vonne Elaine Clements

About the Author
Y'vonne Clements

Being the great-grandmother of four generations of girls is truly extraordinary.

In my life, I have overcome personal challenges that made me realise, I can achieve beyond my own expectations.

In 2000, I decided to write a children's book about mermaids, inspired by grandchildren and featuring a young mermaid named after my granddaughter, T-Naya. This would give my granddaughter great pride in her unique name and fill my spare time with the adventures of the four mermaids. Writing became my happy place.

On completion of the book, I realised that publishing was out of my reach and felt overwhelmed at the possibility of self-publishing. However, 20 years later, my life changed forever, prompting me to seize the moment and complete the story I once started.

Diagnosed with inoperable cancer, I revisited writing as a way to calm my anxiety and entertain my uncertain and frightened mind. My heart needed a new direction and rediscovering T-Naya's story was just the recipe to get me through my biggest challenge.

Thanks to my strength and the help of Bowerbird Publishing, my story will be read not only by T-Naya but many mermaid-loving children.